Words to Know Before You Read

crawled

desert

grumbling

loping

meercat

ostrich

raindrop

tortoise

tunnel

www.rourkeeducationalmedia.com

Edited by Luana K. Mitten
Illustrated by Robin Koontz
Art Direction and Page Layout by Renee Brady

Library of Congress Cataloging-in-Publication Data

Koontz, Robin
Lizzie Little, The Sky is Falling! / Robin Koontz.
    p. cm. -- (Little Birdie Books)
ISBN 978-1-61741-825-9 (hard cover) (alk. paper)
ISBN 978-1-61236-029-4 (soft cover)
Library of Congress Control Number: 2011924706

Printed in China, FOFO I - Production Company
  Shenzhen, Guangdong Province

Rourke
Educational Media

rourkeeducationalmedia.com

customerservice@rourkeeducationalmedia.com • PO Box 643328 Vero Beach, Florida 32964

LIZZIE LITTLE,

The Sky is Falling!

Written and Illustrated by

Robin Koontz

Lizzie Lizard was sunning herself on a rock. Splat! Something hit her head. Lizzie looked all around. The desert looked empty.

Splat! Something hit her head again.
"The sky is falling!" cried Lizzie.
She leaped off her rock and ran.

Missy Meercat came loping up behind her. "Where are you going in such a big rush?" asked Missy.

"The sky is falling!" cried Lizzie. "I am going to tell the king."

"I'll go with you," said Missy.

Ozzie Ostrich came trotting up behind them. "Where are you two going in such a mad dash?" asked Ozzie.

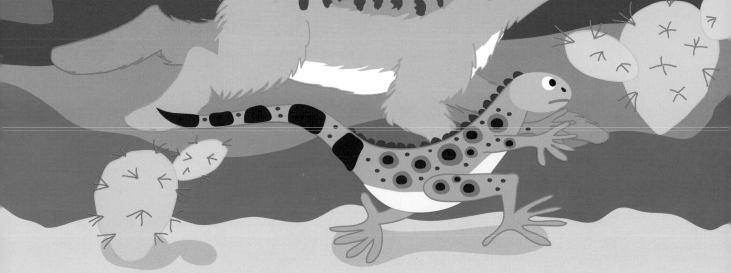

"The sky is falling!" they cried. "We are going to tell the king."

"I'll go with you," said Ozzie.

9

They stopped in front of Jakey Snakey.
"Where are you all going in such a hurry?" he hissed.

"The sky is falling!" they cried. "We are going to tell the king."

"Let me show you a *sss*-shortcut," said Jakey.

Lizzy, Missy, and Ozzie followed Jakey to a big hole. "This tunnel leads-*sss* to the king's palace," said Jakey. Just then, Tommy Tortoise crawled from behind a big rock.

"Don't go in there!" Tommy cried. "It's a TRAP! Jakey is just looking for lunch."

Jakey Snakey *sss*-slithered away, hissing and grumbling.

"Thank you," said Lizzy. "But we have to see the king right away!"

"Why?" Tommy asked.

"Because the sky is falling!" they all cried.

Splat! Lizzie felt something hit her head.
"There it is again!" she cried.

"That was a raindrop," said Tommy.

"What is a raindrop?" asked Lizzie.

"Raindrops make desert flowers bloom," said Tommy. "I guess you are too young to know about rain." Tommy lumbered off as rain began to fall.

"Let's go look at the desert flowers," said Missy.

The new friends set off on their first desert flower tour.

After Reading Activities

You and the Story...

Where did this story take place?

Why were all the animals trying to get to the king?

What would you do if someone said the sky was falling?

After finishing the story tell a friend what you think happened next.

Words You Know Now...

Write each word on a piece of paper and then think of a new word with the same beginning sound.

crawled   ostrich
desert   raindrop
grumbling   tortoise
loping   tunnel
meercat

You Could...Plan Your Own Nature Walk

• Decide where you would like to go on a walk.

• Create a journal for your nature walk.
  - Make a list of what you want to look for on your walk.

• Pack a backpack with supplies.
  - Water bottle
  - Camera
  - Plastic for collecting
  - Journal
  - Pencil

• Set a time for your walk and invite a friend to go with you. (Make sure to let an adult know you are going.)

Enjoy your walk and always remember safety first!

About the Author and Illustrator

Robin Koontz loves to write and illustrate stories that make kids laugh. Robin lives with her husband and various critters in the Coast Range mountains of western Oregon. She shares her office space with Jeep the dog, who gives her most of her ideas.